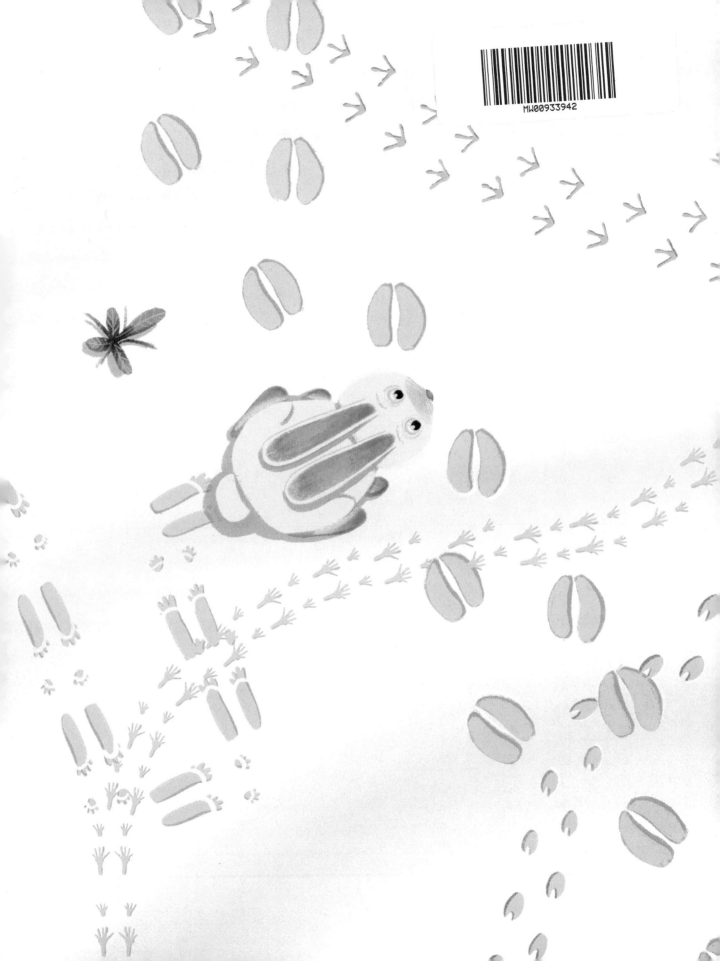

Share Share Ms. Hare

ISBN: 978-1-951597-26-9 (paperback)
ISBN: 978-1-951597-27-6 (ebook)

Library of Congress Control Number: 2021900764

Illustrations by Margherita Grasso
Editing by Laura Boffa, Jana Broecker, Sam Pendlelton

First printing edition 2021.

Free Kids Press

Visit www.authorbcummings.com

Share Share MS. HARE

Written by
Becky Cummings

Illustrated by
Margherita Grasso

FREE KIDS
PRESS

As the animals woke up, the farm was filled with joy. They found their brown dirt pens covered in fluffy white snow! Mouse was the first to squeak about it.

"Winter is here. Come see the snow!" Mouse shouted at the Rooster, who was still half asleep.

He let out the loudest cock-a-doodle-do to spread the word. "Attention, everyone! Goats and pigs and turkeys too, I have advice to give to you. Cold has come! So let's prepare. Grab your hay and fluff your hair!"
Rooster closed his eyes and fell peacefully back asleep.

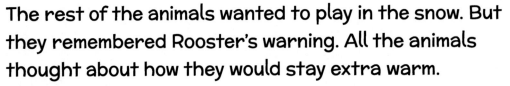

The rest of the animals wanted to play in the snow. But they remembered Rooster's warning. All the animals thought about how they would stay extra warm.

Ms. Hare turned to Mouse and said with a proud grin, "I'm ready to go out! My fluff keeps me toasty. But you'd better bundle up or you'll become a mousicle."

At breakfast time, Mouse thought about how she could stay warm like Ms. Hare. She decided to ask her for a tiny favor.

"Oh Ms. Hare, would you be so kind to let me comb you a little? With a bit of your hair, I can make a coat to keep me warm," asked Mouse with a sweet smile.

Ms. Hare, being the giving friend that she was, allowed
Mouse to gently comb her. Mouse used the hair to make
a coat. Then, she scooted into the snow to make tunnels.

At snack time, Goat thought about how he could stay warm like Mouse. He decided to ask Ms. Hare for a tiny favor.

"Oh Ms. Hare, would you be so kind to let me cut a little bit of your hair? I want to make horn warmers," asked Goat with a look of love.

Ms. Hare, being the giving friend that she was, allowed Goat to give her a small haircut. He used the hair to make a delightful set of horn warmers. Then, Goat galloped into the snow to make goat angels.

At lunch time, Turkey thought about how he could stay warm like Goat and Mouse. He decided to ask Ms. Hare for a tiny favor.

"Oh Ms. Hare, would you be so kind to let me shave off a little of your hair? I need boots," asked Turkey with pleading eyes.

Ms. Hare, being the giving friend that she was, allowed Turkey to shave a strip of hair off her back and use it for cozy boots. Then, Turkey trotted off into the snow to make boot prints.

At dinner time, the pigs noticed all the animals' new winter gear. They thought about how they could stay warm like Turkey, Goat, and Mouse. The pigs decided to ask Ms. Hare for a tiny favor.

"Oh Ms. Hare, would you be so kind to let us buzz off a little of your hair to make scarves?" asked the pig with begging hooves.

Ms. Hare, being the giving friend that she was, allowed the pigs to take the rest of her hair and use it to make thick scarves. Then, the pigs frolicked into the snow to make snowballs.

All the animals played happily in the snow.

Not Ms. Hare, though. She was too tired and hungry from all her sharing. She decided to grab a drink of water and a carrot. When she reached the water trough, she saw her reflection.

"Oh no! What have I done?" shrieked Ms. Hare. "I love sharing, but this has gone too far. How will I stay warm now?"

She decided to call it a night and think it over. She had to bury herself deep under the hay to stay cozy.

Ms. Hare had just about fallen asleep when she felt a tug on her tail. She looked up and saw Cow's big sticky tongue.

"OUCH! What are you doing? That's my tail," she shouted.

Cow looked startled. "Ms. Hare! Oh no. I didn't realize it was you under that hay. I saw a fluffy ball and thought I could use it to make a warm earmuff. I'm so sorry."

"It's okay," said Ms. Hare. "I know I don't look myself. I gave away all my fur and now I need to find a way to stay warm." She decided to call a farm meeting.

"Cow, can you moo everyone together?" Ms. Hare requested. The animals slowly gathered, exhausted from playing in the snow.

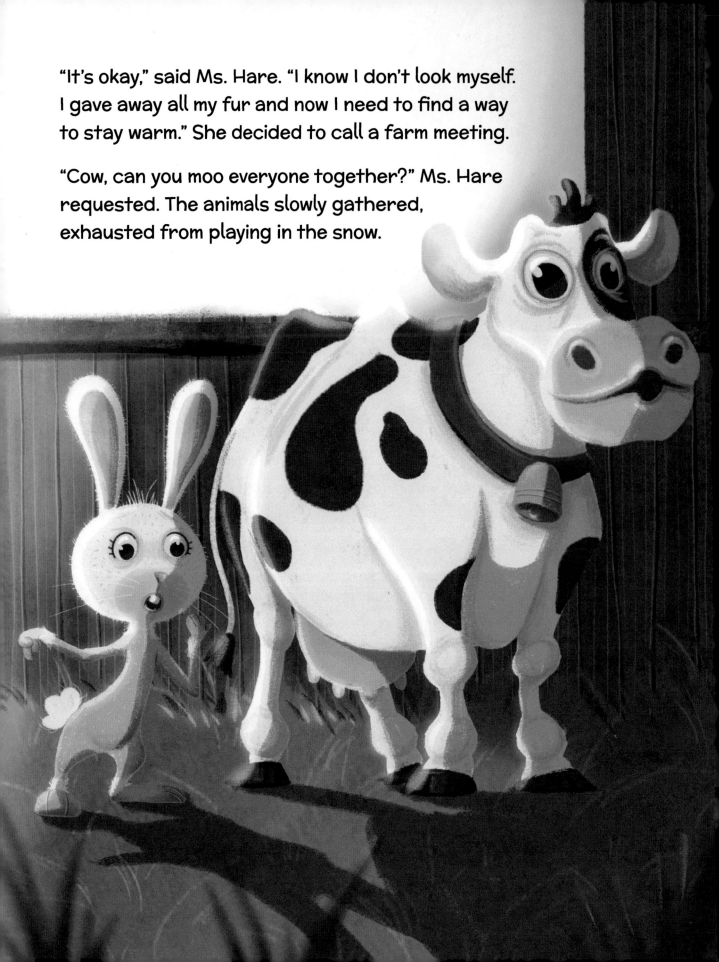

"Feathered and furry friends, today I was trying to be kind to all," said Ms. Hare. "Giving is great, but this went too far. Our hair and feathers belong on our own bodies. Now I know how important it is to take care of myself first."

Goat shook his head in agreement and
the warmers popped off. The pigs sadly
lowered their heads and slid off their scarves.
Turkey took off his boots. Mouse said, "You are right.
We are sorry we took your hair. We will make you a
special coat to wear until it grows back."

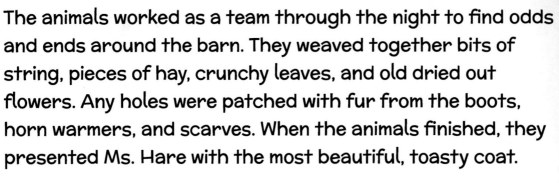

The animals worked as a team through the night to find odds and ends around the barn. They weaved together bits of string, pieces of hay, crunchy leaves, and old dried out flowers. Any holes were patched with fur from the boots, horn warmers, and scarves. When the animals finished, they presented Ms. Hare with the most beautiful, toasty coat.

"Thank you, my friends. Not only have you warmed my body, but you have warmed my heart too."

If you enjoyed this book, be sure to check out my other books!

Becky

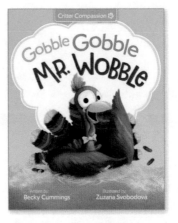

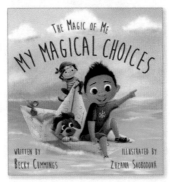

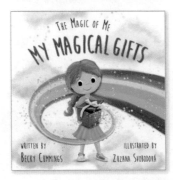

Visit www.authorbcummings.com

Becky Cummings is an author, teacher and mom of three. She loves kids and speaking her truth. Becky is blessed to combine these passions by writing children's books that spread messages of love, hope, faith, health, and happiness. When she isn't writing, you might find her salsa dancing, eating a veggie burrito at her favorite Mexican joint, or traveling to new places! Becky is available for author visits and wants to connect with you.

Margherita Grasso is an illustrator and graphic designer, living and working in Milan, Italy. She loves to represent the world around her with colors and humor. Where there is a shadow, there's a light too: in all her illustrations the light and its reflections are the protagonists. She likes focusing on those details that can be noticed only by sharp eyes. It may sound insignificant, but maybe the idea started just from there! instagram.com/margherita_grasso

I hope the story about Ms. Hare made you laugh as she gave away all her fur and became hairless. As silly as it seems, this story addresses a serious problem in our world. Right now, there are businesses that raise animals in cages so that their fur or skin can be used for clothing, furniture, or other items. Many shoes, wallets, purses, coats, couches, chairs, and belts are made from animal parts.

You can help save animals' lives by being a smart shopper. This means that when you or your parents buy things, you ask this important question: Did an animal get hurt or have to die for this item to be made? If the answer is yes, then don't buy it. There are many options to buy things that look like leather, fur, or animal skin, but aren't made with animal parts. This way, you can still wear something to celebrate the beauty of animals and do no harm.

Made in the USA
Coppell, TX
11 September 2022